SCARY
FAIRY TALES

The Ogre of Rashomon
and Other Stories

COMPILED BY VIC PARKER

Gareth Stevens
PUBLISHING

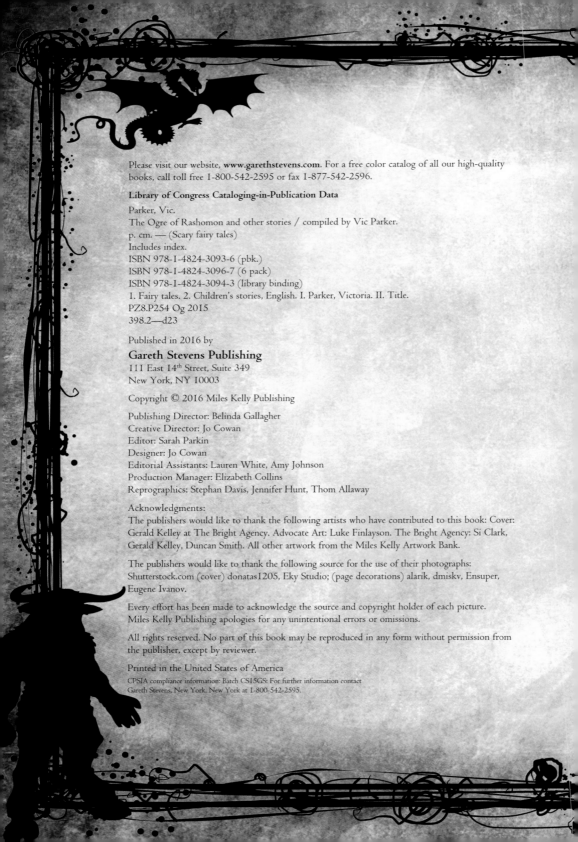

Please visit our website, **www.garethstevens.com**. For a free color catalog of all our high-quality books, call toll free 1-800-542-2595 or fax 1-877-542-2596.

Library of Congress Cataloging-in-Publication Data

Parker, Vic.
The Ogre of Rashomon and other stories / compiled by Vic Parker.
p. cm. — (Scary fairy tales)
Includes index.
ISBN 978-1-4824-3093-6 (pbk.)
ISBN 978-1-4824-3096-7 (6 pack)
ISBN 978-1-4824-3094-3 (library binding)
1. Fairy tales. 2. Children's stories, English. I. Parker, Victoria. II. Title.
PZ8.P254 Og 2015
398.2—d23

Published in 2016 by

Gareth Stevens Publishing
111 East 14th Street, Suite 349
New York, NY 10003

Copyright © 2016 Miles Kelly Publishing

Publishing Director: Belinda Gallagher
Creative Director: Jo Cowan
Editor: Sarah Parkin
Designer: Jo Cowan
Editorial Assistants: Lauren White, Amy Johnson
Production Manager: Elizabeth Collins
Reprographics: Stephan Davis, Jennifer Hunt, Thom Allaway

Acknowledgments:
The publishers would like to thank the following artists who have contributed to this book: Cover: Gerald Kelley at The Bright Agency. Advocate Art: Luke Finlayson. The Bright Agency: Si Clark, Gerald Kelley, Duncan Smith. All other artwork from the Miles Kelly Artwork Bank.

The publishers would like to thank the following source for the use of their photographs: Shutterstock.com (cover) donatas1205, Eky Studio; (page decorations) alarik, dmiskv, Ensuper, Eugene Ivanov.

Every effort has been made to acknowledge the source and copyright holder of each picture. Miles Kelly Publishing apologies for any unintentional errors or omissions.

Printed in the United States of America

CPSIA compliance information: Batch CS15GS: For further information contact
Gareth Stevens, New York, New York at 1-800-542-2595.

CONTENTS

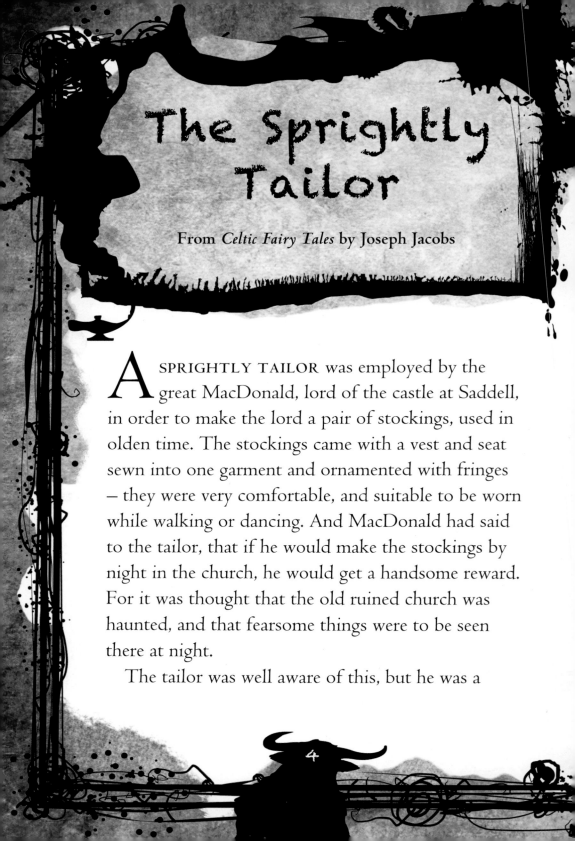

The Sprightly Tailor

From *Celtic Fairy Tales* by Joseph Jacobs

A SPRIGHTLY TAILOR was employed by the great MacDonald, lord of the castle at Saddell, in order to make the lord a pair of stockings, used in olden time. The stockings came with a vest and seat sewn into one garment and ornamented with fringes — they were very comfortable, and suitable to be worn while walking or dancing. And MacDonald had said to the tailor, that if he would make the stockings by night in the church, he would get a handsome reward. For it was thought that the old ruined church was haunted, and that fearsome things were to be seen there at night.

The tailor was well aware of this, but he was a

sprightly man, and when the lord dared him to make the stockings by night in the church, the tailor was not to be daunted, but took it in hand to gain the prize. So, when night came, away he went up the glen, about half a mile distance from the castle, until he came to the old church. Then he chose a nice gravestone for a seat and he lighted his candle, put on his thimble, and set to work at the stockings. He plied his needle nimbly, and thought about the reward that the lord would have to give him.

For some time he got on pretty well, until he felt the floor all of a tremble under his feet. Looking around him, but keeping his fingers at work, he saw the appearance of a great human head rising up through the stone pavement of the church. And when the head had risen above the surface, there came from it a great, great voice. And the voice said, "Do you see this great head of mine?"

"I see that, but I'll sew this!" replied the sprightly tailor, and he stitched away at the stockings.

Then the head rose higher up through the pavement,

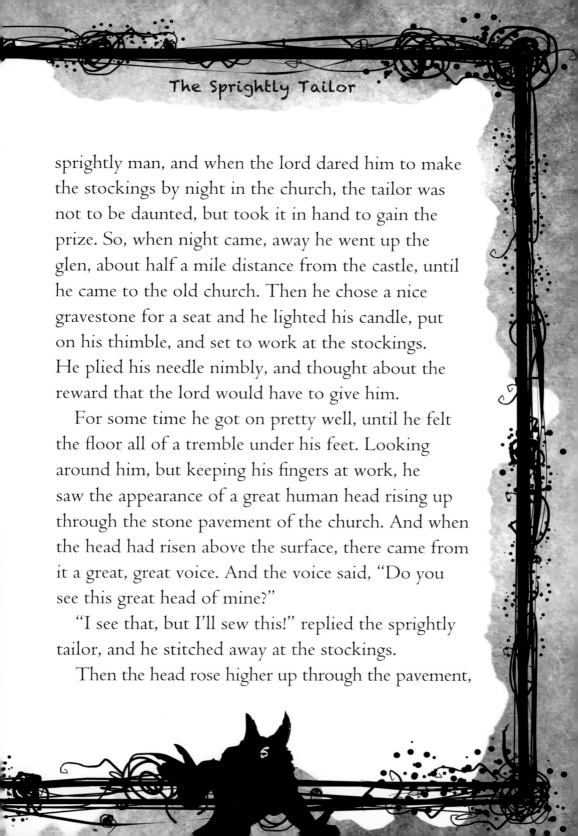

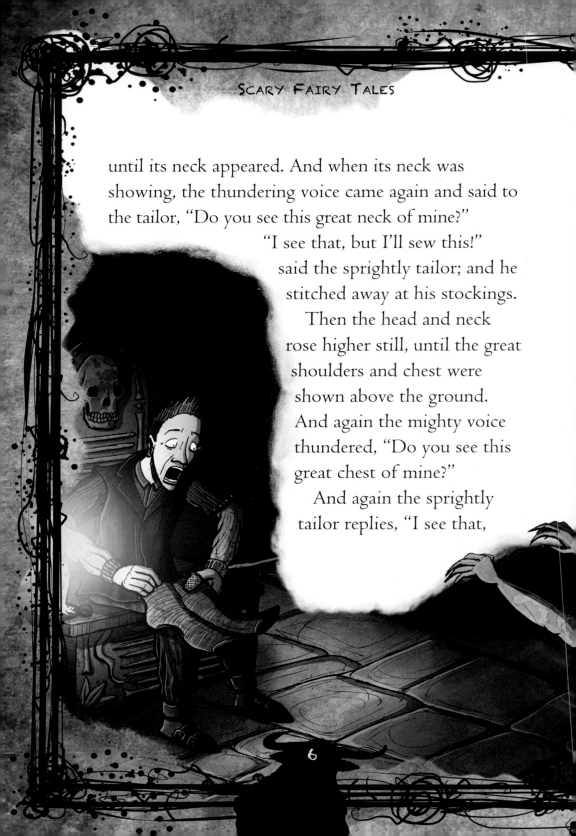

until its neck appeared. And when its neck was showing, the thundering voice came again and said to the tailor, "Do you see this great neck of mine?"

"I see that, but I'll sew this!" said the sprightly tailor; and he stitched away at his stockings.

Then the head and neck rose higher still, until the great shoulders and chest were shown above the ground. And again the mighty voice thundered, "Do you see this great chest of mine?"

And again the sprightly tailor replies, "I see that,

6

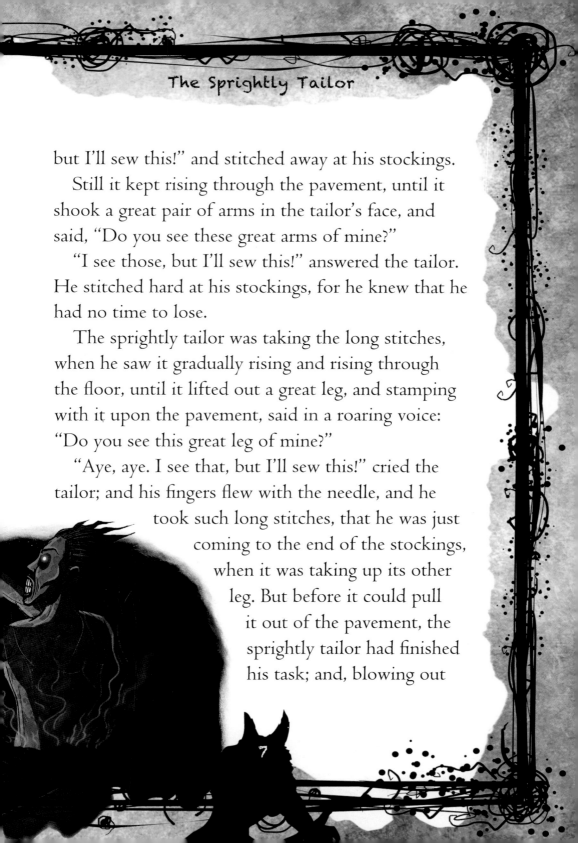

but I'll sew this!" and stitched away at his stockings.

Still it kept rising through the pavement, until it shook a great pair of arms in the tailor's face, and said, "Do you see these great arms of mine?"

"I see those, but I'll sew this!" answered the tailor. He stitched hard at his stockings, for he knew that he had no time to lose.

The sprightly tailor was taking the long stitches, when he saw it gradually rising and rising through the floor, until it lifted out a great leg, and stamping with it upon the pavement, said in a roaring voice: "Do you see this great leg of mine?"

"Aye, aye. I see that, but I'll sew this!" cried the tailor; and his fingers flew with the needle, and he took such long stitches, that he was just coming to the end of the stockings, when it was taking up its other leg. But before it could pull it out of the pavement, the sprightly tailor had finished his task; and, blowing out

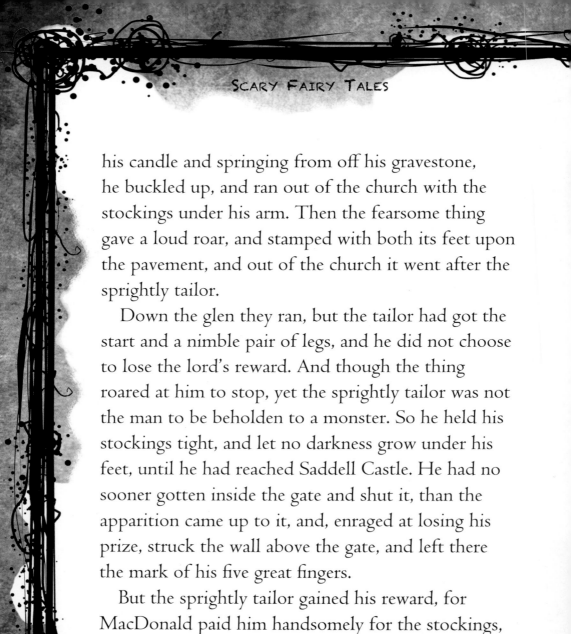

his candle and springing from off his gravestone,
he buckled up, and ran out of the church with the
stockings under his arm. Then the fearsome thing
gave a loud roar, and stamped with both its feet upon
the pavement, and out of the church it went after the
sprightly tailor.

Down the glen they ran, but the tailor had got the
start and a nimble pair of legs, and he did not choose
to lose the lord's reward. And though the thing
roared at him to stop, yet the sprightly tailor was not
the man to be beholden to a monster. So he held his
stockings tight, and let no darkness grow under his
feet, until he had reached Saddell Castle. He had no
sooner gotten inside the gate and shut it, than the
apparition came up to it, and, enraged at losing his
prize, struck the wall above the gate, and left there
the mark of his five great fingers.

But the sprightly tailor gained his reward, for
MacDonald paid him handsomely for the stockings,
and never discovered that a few of the stitches
were long.

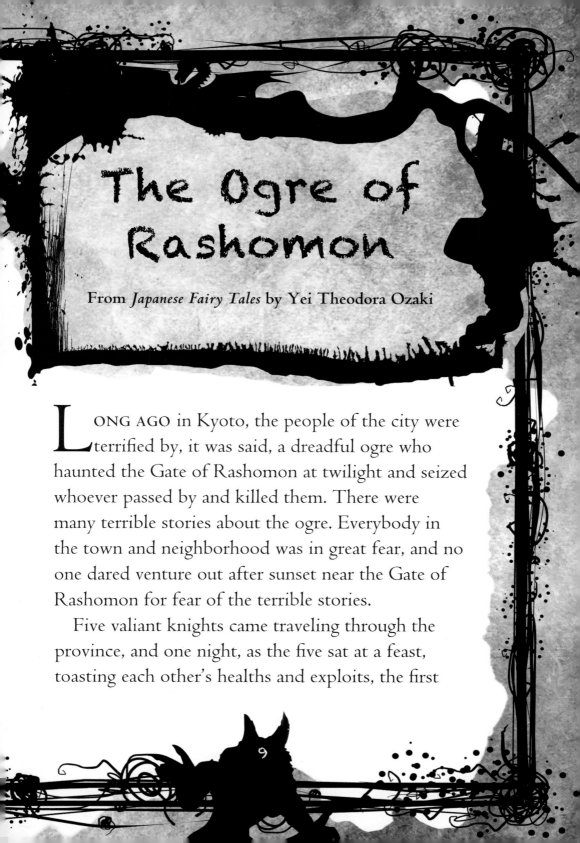

The Ogre of Rashomon

From *Japanese Fairy Tales* by Yei Theodora Ozaki

LONG AGO in Kyoto, the people of the city were terrified by, it was said, a dreadful ogre who haunted the Gate of Rashomon at twilight and seized whoever passed by and killed them. There were many terrible stories about the ogre. Everybody in the town and neighborhood was in great fear, and no one dared venture out after sunset near the Gate of Rashomon for fear of the terrible stories.

Five valiant knights came traveling through the province, and one night, as the five sat at a feast, toasting each other's healths and exploits, the first

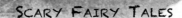

knight, Hojo, said to the others: "Have you heard the rumors about the ogre at the Gate of Rashomon?"

The second knight, Watanabe, answered him, saying, "Do not talk such nonsense! There is no longer such thing as ogres."

"Then go there yourself and find out whether it is true or not," said Hojo.

Watanabe, the second knight, could not bear the thought that his companion should believe he was afraid, so he at once got ready to go — he buckled on his long sword and put on a coat of armor, and tied on his large helmet. When he was ready to start he said to the others, "Give me something so that I can prove I have been there!" Then one of the men got a roll of writing paper and his box of Indian ink and brushes, and the four friends wrote their names on a piece of paper. "I will take this," said Watanabe, "and put it on the Gate of Rashomon, so tomorrow morning you will all go and look at it. I may be able to catch an ogre or two by then!" and he mounted his horse and rode off gallantly.

It was a moonless and stormy night, but Watanabe sped on and at last he reached the Gate of Rashomon. Peer as he might through the darkness he could see no sign of an ogre. "It is just as I thought," said Watanabe to himself, "there are certainly no ogres here; it is only an old woman's story. I will stick this paper on the gate so that the others can see I have been here when they come tomorrow, and then I will make my way home and laugh at them all." He fastened the piece of paper, signed by all his four companions, on the gate, and then turned his horse's head towards home.

As he did so, his helmet was seized from the back. "Who are you?" cried Watanabe fearlessly. He then put out his hand and groped around to find out who or what it was that held him by the helmet. As he did so he touched something that felt like an arm – it was covered with hair and was as big round as the trunk of a tree!

Watanabe knew at once that this was the arm of an ogre, so he drew his sword and cut at it fiercely.

There was a loud yell of pain, and then the ogre
dashed in front of the warrior. Watanabe's eyes grew
large with wonder, for he saw that the ogre was taller
than the great gate, his eyes
were flashing like mirrors

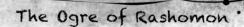

in the sunlight, and his huge mouth was wide open, and as the monster breathed, flames of fire shot out of his mouth.

Watanabe never flinched. He attacked the ogre with all his strength, and thus they fought face to face for a long time. At last the ogre, finding that he could neither frighten nor beat Watanabe and that he might himself be beaten, took off. But Watanabe, determined not to let the monster escape, put spurs to his horse and gave chase. But though the knight rode very fast the ogre ran faster, and to his disappointment he found himself unable to overtake the monster, who was gradually lost to sight.

Watanabe returned to the gate where the fierce fight had taken place, and got down from his horse. As he did so he stumbled upon something lying on the ground. Stooping to pick it up he found that it was one of the ogre's huge arms, which he must have slashed off in the fight. His joy was great at having secured such a prize, for this was the best of all proofs of his adventure with the ogre. So he took it

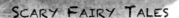

up and carried it home as a trophy of his victory.

When he got back, he showed the arm to his friends, who one and all called him the hero of their band and gave him a great feast. His wonderful deed was soon noised abroad in Kyoto, and people from far and near came to see the ogre's arm.

Watanabe now began to grow uneasy as to how he should keep the arm in safety, for he knew that the ogre to whom it belonged was still alive. He felt sure that one day or other, as soon as the ogre got over his scare, he would come to try to get his arm back again. Watanabe therefore had a box made of the strongest wood and banded with iron. In this he placed the arm, and then he sealed down the heavy lid, refusing to open it for anyone. He kept the box in his own room and took charge of it himself, never allowing it out of his sight.

Now one night he heard someone knocking at the porch, asking for admittance. When the servant went to the door to see who it was, there was only an old woman, very respectable in appearance. When she

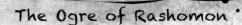

was asked who she was and what was her business, the old woman replied with a smile that she had been nurse to the master of the house when he was a little baby. If the lord of the house were at home she begged to be allowed to see him.

The servant left the old woman at the door and went to tell his master that his old nurse had come to see him. Watanabe thought it strange that she should come at that time of night. But at the thought of his old nurse, who had been like a foster mother to him and whom he had not seen for a long time, a very tender feeling sprang up for her in his heart. He ordered the servant to show her in.

The old woman was ushered into the room, and after the customary bows and greetings were over, she said, "Master, the report of your brave fight with the ogre at the Gate of Rashomon is so widely known that even your poor old nurse has heard of it. I am very proud to think that my master was so brave as to dare to cut off an ogre's arm. Before I die it is the great wish of my life to see this arm."

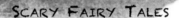

"No," said Watanabe, "I am sorry, but I cannot grant your request. Ogres are very vengeful creatures, and if I open the box there is no telling but that he may suddenly appear and carry off his arm."

The woman pleaded and pleaded, but Watanabe still refused.

Then the old woman said, "Do you suspect me of being a spy sent by the ogre?"

"No, of course I do not suspect you of being the ogre's spy, for you are my old nurse," Watanabe answered her.

"Then you cannot refuse to show me the arm any longer," pleaded the old woman, "for it is the great wish of my heart to see for once in my life the arm of an ogre!"

Watanabe could not hold out in his refusal any longer, so he gave in at last. And he led the way to his own room, the old woman following.

When they were both in the room Watanabe shut the door carefully, and then going towards a big box which stood in a corner of the room, he took off the heavy lid and called the old woman to come near.

"What is it like? Let me have a good look at it," said the old nurse, with a joyful face.

She came nearer and nearer, as if she were afraid, until she stood right against the box. Suddenly she plunged her hand into the box and seized the arm, crying with a fearful voice which made the room

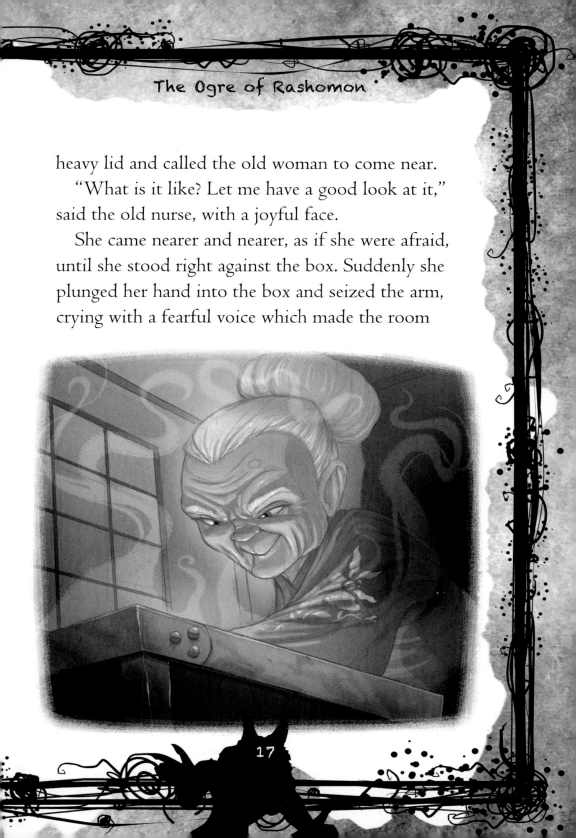

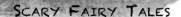
shake: "Oh, joy! I have got my arm back again!" And from an old woman she was suddenly transformed into the towering figure of the frightful ogre!

Watanabe sprang back and was unable to move for a moment, so great was his astonishment, but recognizing the ogre who had attacked him, he determined with his usual courage to put an end to him this time. He seized his sword, drew it out of its sheath in a flash, and tried to cut the ogre down.

So quick was Watanabe that the creature had a narrow escape. But the ogre sprang up to the ceiling and, bursting through the roof, disappeared in the mist and clouds.

The knight waited in patience for another opportunity to dispatch the ogre. But the latter was afraid of Watanabe's great strength and daring, and never troubled Kyoto again. So once more the people of the city were able to go out without fear even at nighttime, and the brave deeds of Watanabe have never been forgotten!

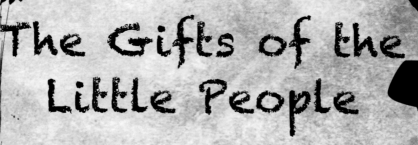

The Gifts of the Little People

By the Brothers Grimm

A TAILOR AND A GOLDSMITH were journeying together when one evening, just as the sun had sunk behind the mountains, they heard the sound of distant music. It had a strange sound, but was so pleasing that they forgot their weariness and walked speedily ahead. The moon had already risen when they arrived at a hill, upon which they viewed a large number of small men and women, who were holding hands and dancing around and cheerfully singing with the greatest pleasure and happiness. That was the music that the wanderers had heard.

An old man, somewhat larger than the others, sat in their midst. He wore a brightly colored jacket, and his ice-gray beard hung down over his chest. Filled with amazement, the two wanderers stopped and watched the dance. The old man motioned to them that they too should join in, and the little people voluntarily opened their circle.

The goldsmith, who had a hump on his back but was bold rather than self-conscious, stepped right up. The tailor was at first a little shy and held back, but as soon as he saw what fun it was, he too took heart and joined in.

They closed the circle again, and the little people sang and danced wildly. However, the old man took a broad knife that had been hanging from his belt, sharpened it, and looked at the strangers. They were frightened, but they did not have to worry for long. The old man grabbed the goldsmith and with the greatest speed smoothly shaved off his beard and the hair from his head. Then the same thing happened to the tailor. Their fear disappeared when the old man patted them friendly on their shoulders, as if to say that they had done well by letting it all happen without resisting. With his finger he pointed toward a pile of coal that lay nearby, and indicated to them through gestures that they should fill their pockets with it. They both obeyed, although they did not know of what use the coal would be to them. Then they went on their way to seek out a place to spend the night.

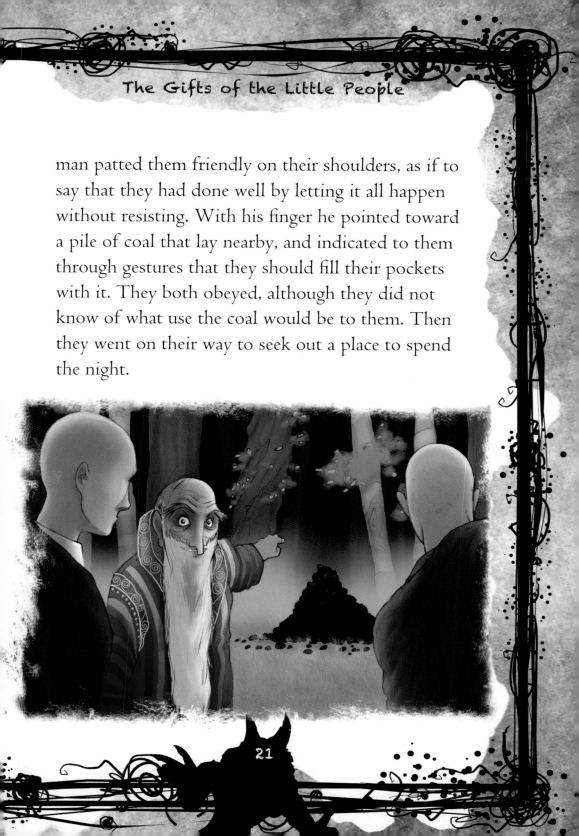

They had just arrived in a valley when the bell from a neighboring monastery struck twelve. The distant sound of the little people's singing ceased instantly. The two wanderers found shelter. Lying on beds of straw, they covered themselves with their jackets. They were so tired that they forgot to take the coal out of their pockets first.

They were awakened earlier than normal by a heavy weight pressing down on their limbs. They reached into their pockets, and could hardly believe their eyes when they saw that they were not filled with coal, but with pure gold. Further, their hair and their beards had also been fully restored.

Now they were rich. However, the goldsmith had twice as much as the tailor, because — true to his greedy nature — he had filled his pockets better. However much a greedy person has, he always wants more, so the goldsmith proposed to the tailor that they stay there another day, in order to be able to gain even more wealth from the old man on the mountain that evening.

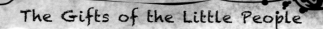

The tailor did not want to do this, and said, "I have enough and am satisfied. I am going to become a master, marry my sweetheart, and be a happy man." However, to please the goldsmith, he agreed to stay one more day.

That evening the goldsmith hung several sacks over his shoulders in order to be able to carry everything, and set off for the hill. As had happened the night before, he found the little people dancing and singing. The old man shaved him smooth once again, and indicated that he should take some coal. Without hesitating he packed away as much as his pockets and sacks would hold, and then happily returned home. Covering himself with his jacket he said: "I can bear it, if the gold presses down on me." With the sweet idea that he would awaken tomorrow as a very rich man, he fell asleep.

When he opened his eyes, he got up quickly in order to examine his pockets. How astounded he was, that he pulled out nothing but black coal, no matter how often he reached inside. "Anyway, I still

have the gold from the night before," he thought, and reached for it. Horrified, he saw that it too had turned back into coal. He struck himself on the forehead with his grimy hand, and felt that his entire head was as bald and smooth as his beardless chin.

Nor was that the end of his misfortune. He suddenly noticed that in addition to the hump on his back, a second one, of the same size, had grown on his chest. Now he recognized the punishment for his greed and began to cry aloud.

The good tailor, who had been awakened by all this, consoled the unhappy man as best he could, saying: "You were my traveling companion, and you can stay with me now and live from my treasure."

He kept his word, but the poor goldsmith had to bear two humps and cover his bald head with a cap as long as he lived.

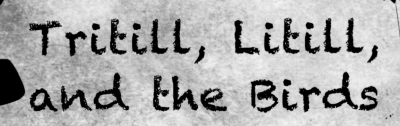

Tritill, Litill, and the Birds

From Andrew Lang's *Crimson Fairy Book*

O NCE UPON A TIME there lived a princess who was so beautiful and so good that everybody loved her. Her father almost died of grief when, one day, she disappeared, and though the whole kingdom was searched, she could not be found in any corner of it. In despair, the king ordered that whoever could find her should have her for his wife. This made the young men search again, but they were no more successful than before, and returned sorrowfully to their homes.

Now there dwelled, not far from the palace, a man

and a wife who had three sons. The two eldest were allowed by their parents to do just as they liked, but the youngest was always obliged to give way to his brothers. When they were all grown up, the eldest told his father that he meant to go away and see the world. The old people were very unhappy, but they said nothing, and began to prepare for his travels. When everything was ready, he bade them farewell.

He walked for miles through a forest and came out on a bare hillside. Here he sat down to rest and, pulling out his napsack, prepared to eat his dinner. He had only eaten a few mouthfuls when an old man, badly dressed, passed by and, seeing the food, asked if the young man could not spare him a little.

"Not I, indeed!" he answered. "Why I have scarcely enough for myself. If you want food you must earn it."

And the beggar went on.

After the young man had finished his dinner he walked on for several hours, until he reached a second hill, where he threw himself down on the grass, and took some bread and milk from his wallet. While he was eating and drinking, there came an old man, yet more wretched than the first, and begged for a few mouthfuls. But instead of food he only got hard words, and limped sadly away.

Towards evening the young man reached an open space in the wood, and by this time he thought he would like some supper. The birds saw the food, and flew round his head hoping for some crumbs, but he threw stones at them and frightened them off. Then he began to wonder where he should sleep. Not where he was, for that was bare and cold, and though he had walked a long way and was tired, he dragged himself up and went on seeking for a shelter.

In the distance, he saw a deep sort of hole or cave

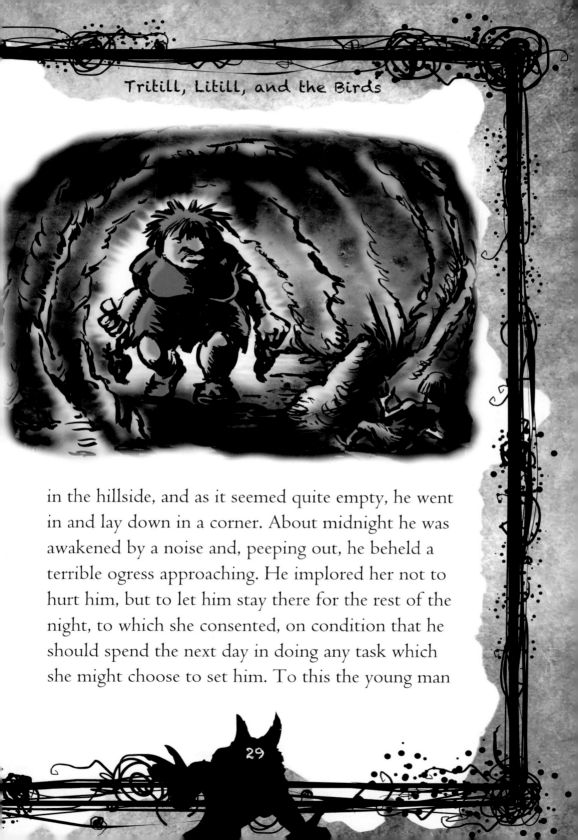

in the hillside, and as it seemed quite empty, he went
in and lay down in a corner. About midnight he was
awakened by a noise and, peeping out, he beheld a
terrible ogress approaching. He implored her not to
hurt him, but to let him stay there for the rest of the
night, to which she consented, on condition that he
should spend the next day in doing any task which
she might choose to set him. To this the young man

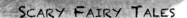

agreed, and turned over and went to sleep again.

In the morning, the ogress bade him sweep the dust out of the cave, and to have it clean before her return in the evening, otherwise it would be the worse for him. Then she left.

The young man began to clean the floor of the cave, but try as he would to move it, the dirt still stuck to its place. He soon gave up the task and sat sulkily in the corner, wondering what punishment the ogress would find for him and why she had set him to do such an impossible thing.

He had not long to wait, after the ogress came home, before he knew what his punishment was to be! She just gave one look at the floor of the cave, then dealt him a blow on the head which cracked his skull, and there was an end of him.

Meanwhile his next brother grew tired of staying at home and let his parents have no rest until they had consented that he also should go out to see the world. He also met the two old beggars, who prayed for a little of his bread and milk, but this young man

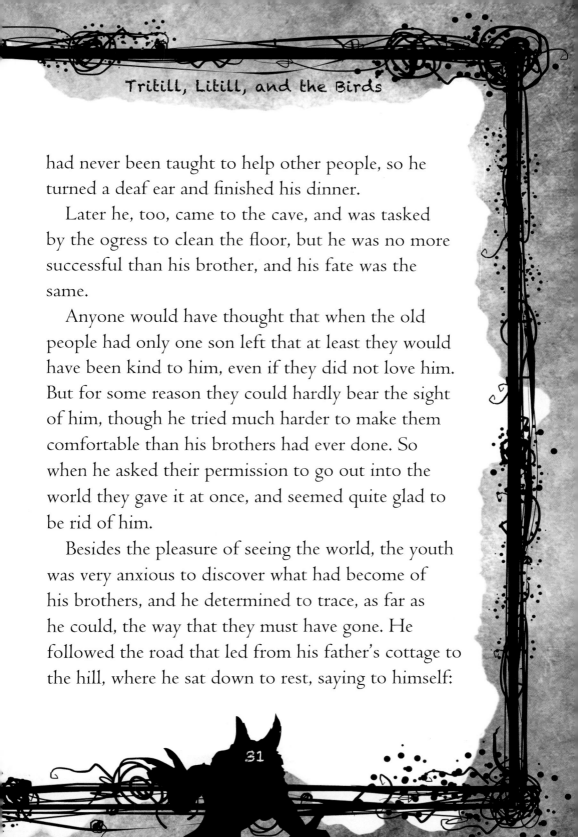

had never been taught to help other people, so he turned a deaf ear and finished his dinner.

Later he, too, came to the cave, and was tasked by the ogress to clean the floor, but he was no more successful than his brother, and his fate was the same.

Anyone would have thought that when the old people had only one son left that at least they would have been kind to him, even if they did not love him. But for some reason they could hardly bear the sight of him, though he tried much harder to make them comfortable than his brothers had ever done. So when he asked their permission to go out into the world they gave it at once, and seemed quite glad to be rid of him.

Besides the pleasure of seeing the world, the youth was very anxious to discover what had become of his brothers, and he determined to trace, as far as he could, the way that they must have gone. He followed the road that led from his father's cottage to the hill, where he sat down to rest, saying to himself:

"I am sure my brothers must have stopped here, and I will do the same."

He was hungry as well as tired, and took out some food. He was just going to begin to eat when the old man appeared. The young man at once broke off some of the bread, begging the old man to sit down beside him, and treating him as if he was an old friend. At last the stranger rose, and said to him: "If ever you are in trouble call me, and I will help you. My name is Tritill." Then he vanished.

At the next hill he met with the second old man, and to him also he gave food and drink. And when this old man had finished he said, like the first: "If you ever want help in the smallest thing call to me. My name is Litill."

The young man walked on until he reached the open space in the wood, where he stopped for supper. In a moment all the birds in the world seemed to be flying around his head, and he crumbled some of his bread for them and watched them dart down to pick it up. When they had cleared off every crumb, the largest bird with the most colorful plumage said to him, "If you are in trouble and need help say, 'My birds, come to me!' and we will come." Then they flew away.

Towards evening the young man reached the cave
where his brothers had met their deaths, and, like
them, he thought it would be a good place to sleep
in. Looking round, he saw some pieces of the dead
men's clothes and of their bones. The sight made him
shiver, but he would not move away, and resolved to
await the return of the ogress, for such he knew she
must be.

Very soon she came striding in, and he asked
politely if she would give him a night's lodging. She
answered as before, that he might stay on condition
that he should do any work that she might set him
to next morning. So the bargain being concluded, the
young man curled himself up in his corner and went
to sleep.

The dirt lay thicker than ever on the floor of the
cave when the young man took the spade and began
his work. He could not clear it any more than his
brothers had done, and at last the spade itself stuck in
the earth so that he could not pull it out. The youth
stared at it in despair, then the old beggar's words

flashed into his mind, and he cried, "Tritill, Tritill, come and help me!"

And Tritill stood beside him and asked what he wanted. The youth told him all his story, and when he had finished, the old man said: "Spade and shovel do your duty," and they danced about the cave till, in a short time, there was not a speck of dust left on the floor. As soon as it was quite clean Tritill went his way.

With a light heart the young man awaited the return of the ogress. When she came in she looked carefully round, and then said to him: "You did not do that quite alone. However, as the floor is clean I will leave your head on."

The following morning the ogress told the young man that he must take all the feathers out of her pillows and spread them to dry in the sun. But if one feather was missing when she came back at night his head should pay for it.

The young man fetched the pillows, and shook out all the feathers, and oh, what quantities of them there

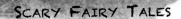
were! Suddenly a breeze sprang up, and in a moment the feathers were dancing high in the air. At first the youth tried to collect them again, but he soon found that it was no use, and he cried in despair: "Tritill, Litill, and my birds, come and help me!"

He had hardly said the words when there they all were; and when the birds had brought all the feathers back again, Tritill and Litill and he put them away in the pillows, as the ogress had bidden him. But one feather they kept out, and told the young man that if the ogress missed it he was to thrust it up her nose. Then they all vanished, Tritill, Litill, and the birds.

As soon as the ogress returned home she flung herself on the bed and the whole cave quivered under her. The pillows were soft and full instead of being empty, which surprised her, but that did not content her. The ogress got up, shook out all of the pillowcases one by one, and began to count the feathers in each. "If one is missing I will have your head," said the ogress.

And at that the young man drew the feather from

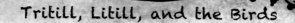

his pocket and thrust it up her nose, crying, "If you want your feather, here it is."

"You did not sort those feathers alone," answered the ogress calmly; "however, I will let that pass."

That night the young man slept soundly, and in the morning the ogress told him that his work that day would be to slay one of her great oxen, to cook its heart, and to make drinking cups of its horns, before she returned home. "There are fifty oxen," added she, "and you must guess which of the herd I want killed. If you guess right, tomorrow you shall be free to go where you will, and you shall choose three things as a reward for your service. But if you slay the wrong ox your head shall pay for it."

When he was left alone, the young man stood thinking for a little. Then he called, "Tritill, Litill, come to my help!"

In a moment he saw them, far away, driving the biggest ox the youth had ever seen. When they drew near, Tritill killed it, Litill took out its heart for the young man to cook, and they both began to quickly turn the horns into drinking cups. The old men warned the youth that he must ask the ogress for the chest which stood at the foot of her bed, for whatever lay on the top of the bed, and for what lay under the

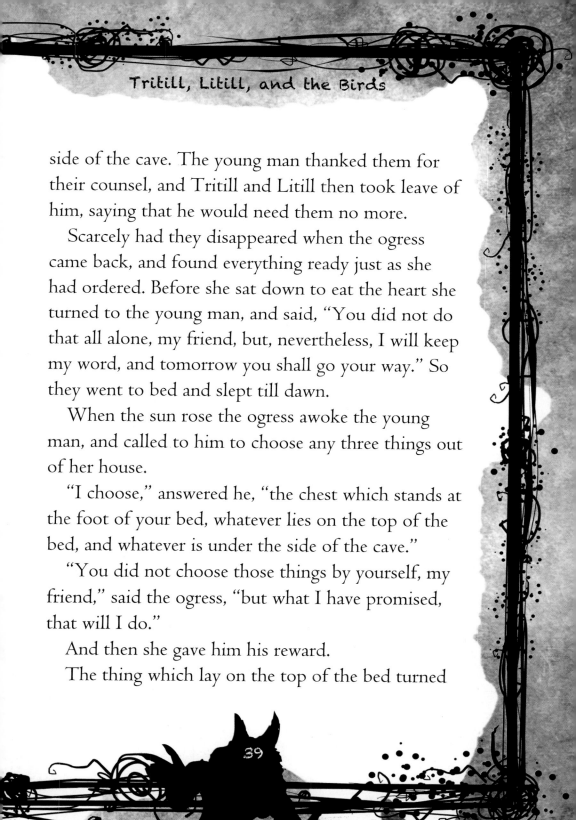

side of the cave. The young man thanked them for their counsel, and Tritill and Litill then took leave of him, saying that he would need them no more.

Scarcely had they disappeared when the ogress came back, and found everything ready just as she had ordered. Before she sat down to eat the heart she turned to the young man, and said, "You did not do that all alone, my friend, but, nevertheless, I will keep my word, and tomorrow you shall go your way." So they went to bed and slept till dawn.

When the sun rose the ogress awoke the young man, and called to him to choose any three things out of her house.

"I choose," answered he, "the chest which stands at the foot of your bed, whatever lies on the top of the bed, and whatever is under the side of the cave."

"You did not choose those things by yourself, my friend," said the ogress, "but what I have promised, that will I do."

And then she gave him his reward.

The thing which lay on the top of the bed turned

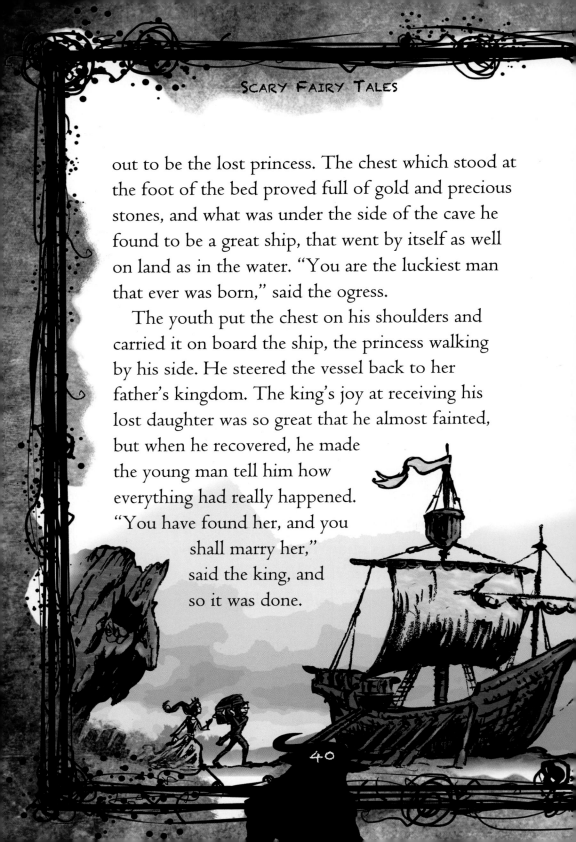

out to be the lost princess. The chest which stood at the foot of the bed proved full of gold and precious stones, and what was under the side of the cave he found to be a great ship, that went by itself as well on land as in the water. "You are the luckiest man that ever was born," said the ogress.

The youth put the chest on his shoulders and carried it on board the ship, the princess walking by his side. He steered the vessel back to her father's kingdom. The king's joy at receiving his lost daughter was so great that he almost fainted, but when he recovered, he made the young man tell him how everything had really happened. "You have found her, and you shall marry her," said the king, and so it was done.